© 1993 Twin Books Ltd

Produced by
TWIN BOOKS
Kimbolton House
117A Fulham Road
London SW3 6RL
England

Directed by CND – Muriel Nathan-Deiller
Illustrated by Van Gool-Lefèvre-Loiseaux

ISBN 1-85469-927-X

Printed in Hong Kong

This edition printed 1994

Jack and the Beanstalk

TWIN BOOKS

Once there was a boy named Jack who lived with his parents in a small country cottage. They worked hard on their farm and were very happy. They had no worries because they possessed three magical treasures: a bag of gold coins that could never be emptied, a little hen that laid golden eggs, and an enchanted harp that played beautiful music.

One day, however, a terrible giant appeared in their land. He frightened children, stole sheep and cattle, and broke down fences and buildings with his huge feet. The giant arrived at Jack's cottage and took the family's magic hen, enchanted harp and bag of gold. Jack's father was so upset that he became very ill, and finally died. Jack and his mother now had to fend for themselves.

Jack and his mother were very poor. They worked harder than before, but a great famine struck the land. One day, when Jack was gathering sticks with his pet squirrel, Chip, his mother called him: "Jack, you must take the cow to market and sell her," she said sadly. "We will use the money for food."

Jack and Chip set off with the cow. On their way, a bird called to them. "I know who will buy your cow," said the bird. "Follow me." So Jack, who enjoyed an adventure, followed the bird into the woods.

The bird perched on the hat of a ragged old man leaning on a staff. "I will buy your cow," he said. "In exchange, I will give you these three magic beans." Jack felt sorry for the old man, and was tempted by the word "magic". He made the exchange and ran home excited, with the beans in his pocket.

"Look, Mother!" cried Jack, rushing into the cottage. "I sold the cow for these magic beans!" But his mother was shocked instead of happy. "What!" she exclaimed. "How will we survive?" "These beans are worthless!" she said throwing them on the ground.

That night, Jack went to bed sad and hungry. But the morning brought a great surprise. The bird he had met the day before flew in through the window and woke him, crying, "Look! Overnight the magic beans have grown into an enormous beanstalk!"

Jack and Chip ran into the
garden. The beanstalk soared
so high above the cottage
that it disappeared into the
clouds. Eager to explore,
Jack began to climb the stalk,
as Chip led the way.

Far up in the clouds, they found a strange land of jagged rocks and rugged cliffs. "I wonder who lives here?" said Jack. The bird guided them to a huge castle in the distance.

"Is anyone at home?" called Jack when they reached the castle. He was amazed when the giant's wife appeared at the door. "Come in quickly and hide," she warned, "before my husband comes home and eats you!" Frightened, Jack and Chip ran into the castle.

The giant's wife was kind and gave Jack something to eat. When he felt better, he looked around in wonder at the huge rooms and large furniture of the castle. "You may stay and rest," said the giant's wife, "but if you hear my husband coming, run away!" Jack was too curious to rest, so he and Chip explored the castle.

Imagine Jack's surprise when he discovered his family's stolen treasures on the giant's table: the magic hen, the enchanted harp and the bag of gold. But as he reached for them, Chip tugged frantically at his shoe. The giant was coming! His thunderous steps shook the castle to its foundations.

Jack dived under the table as the giant stamped into the room, clutching a heavy club. He was suspicious. Sniffing the air, he roared:

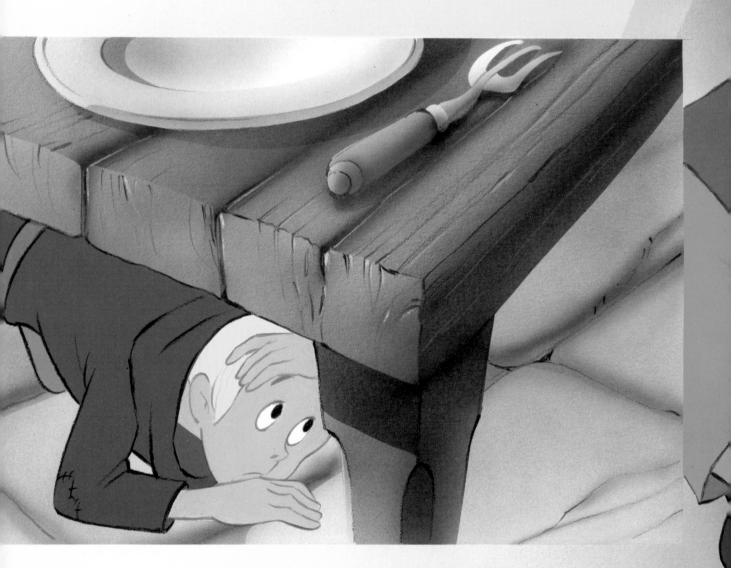

*Fee, fi, fo, fum
I smell the blood of an Englishman!
Be he alive or be he dead
I'll grind his bones to make my bread!*

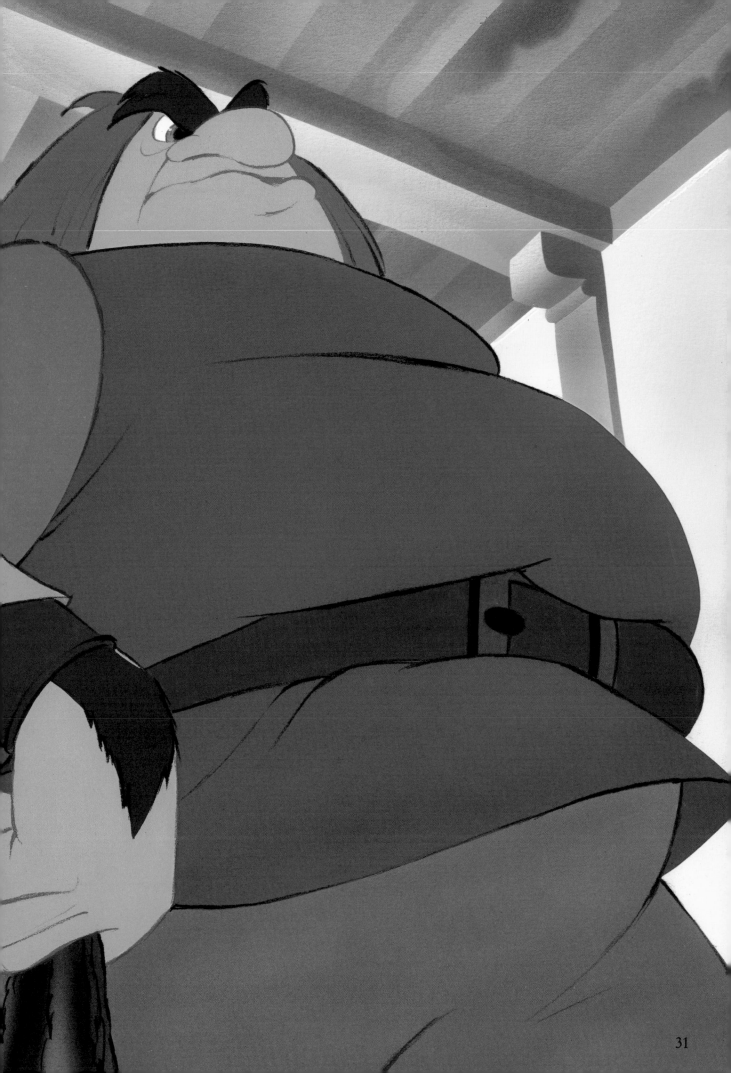

Jack shook with fright, but the giant's wife said, "That's lunch you smell. I have prepared a whole ox. Sit down and eat it before it gets cold." The giant sat down at the table and ate until he could eat no more. Then he began to yawn and stretch. The large meal had made him sleepy. Jack crept from his hiding place, grabbed the bag of gold, and ran to the window.

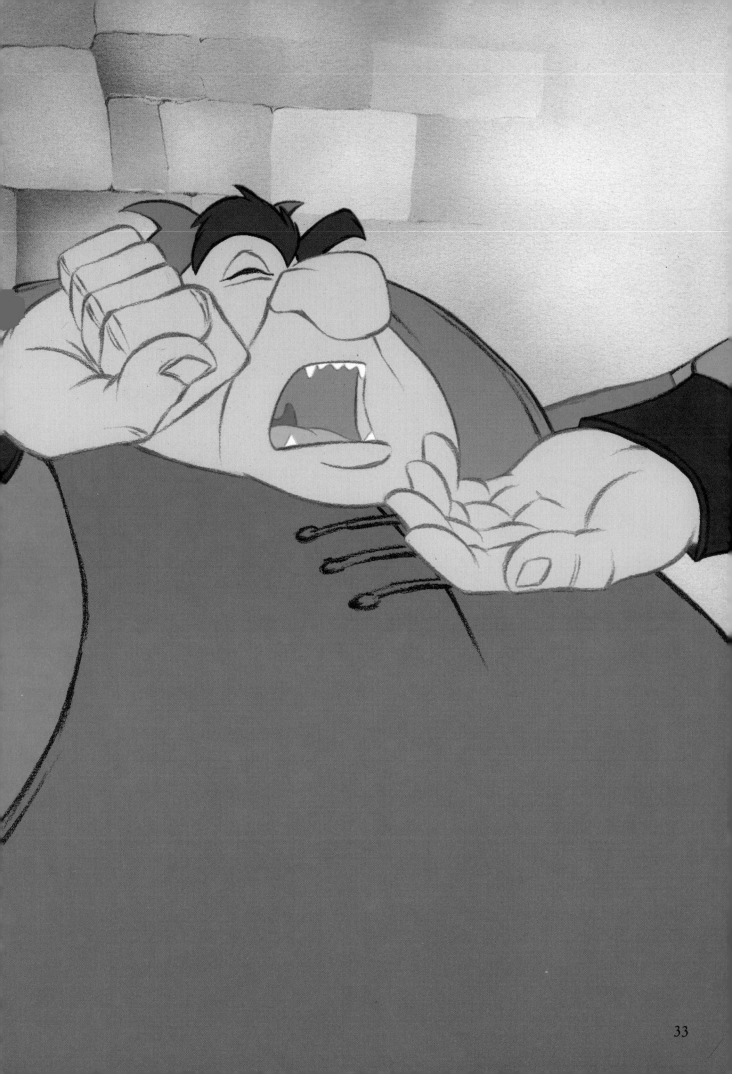

The giant did not wake. Jack and Chip jumped out of the window and ran for their lives. As they approached the beanstalk, they saw their friend, the bird. "Hurry!" he cried, as they leapt in among the leaves and slid rapidly to the ground.

Jack's mother was waiting for him at the foot of the beanstalk. He gave her the bag of gold, saying, "The giant who stole our treasures lives up there! I am going back for the hen and the harp!"

"Wait, Jack!" she cried in alarm. But he was already climbing the beanstalk again. "Don't worry!" he called, and disappeared from sight.

Once again, Jack crept under the table and listened while the giant ate another huge meal. He called to his wife, "Bring me my magic hen. I want one of her golden eggs. Bring my harp as well, so it can play for me." Jack watched from his hiding place.

The moment the giant fell asleep, Jack sprang out and seized the magic hen. With his heart hammering, he sped to the window, grasping her under his arm.

As Jack and Chip jumped out of the window, the hen let out a squawk. They raced across the rocky plain to the beanstalk. Chip tried to calm the frightened hen, but it was too late. The magic hen had woken the sleeping giant!

The ground shook as the giant burst from his castle, swinging his heavy club. Rocks crumbled under his feet, as he searched for the intruders who had run away with his hen and his bag of gold. But Jack and his friend were already tumbling down the beanstalk. The angry giant did not see them.

Jack's mother was so happy to see him back safe that she almost cried. Then her face lit up when she saw the magic hen he had brought home. "We will never be poor again, Mother," said Jack proudly.

But Jack could not stay quietly at home for long. He kept thinking of the enchanted harp in the giant's castle. One morning, he climbed the beanstalk again.

The giant had just called for the harp, and it began to play as Jack and Chip crept into the castle. The harp's beautiful music covered any noise they made. The two friends slid under the table as the harp played a happy tune.

"Play again!" commanded the giant. The harp responded with another burst of sweet music. The sound was so beautiful that Jack and Chip forgot there was any danger and drew closer to listen. The giant spotted them! "You little thieves!" he roared, grabbing his club. Jack snatched the harp and ran as he had never run before.

"Quick!" cried the bird, as they scrambled into the beanstalk. "He's just behind you!" The beanstalk trembled with the giant's weight. Jack almost dropped the harp as he hurried to climb down.

When he reached the ground, Jack seized an axe and struck the base of the beanstalk. He chopped with all his might as the giant swung down hand over hand.

The great beanstalk began to sway back and forth. There was a loud *crack* — and it crashed to the ground. The giant fell and lay motionless in front of the cottage.

"Look, Mother!" cried Jack. "The giant will never frighten anyone again. And now, we have back all the treasures he stole from us." At this, the faithful bird who had guided Jack through all his adventures took flight. His work was done.

The fallen giant sank into the ground, and a lake appeared where the beanstalk had grown so mysteriously in the night. Jack and Chip waved goodbye to the bird and went back into the cottage with light hearts. What excitement they had shared!

Jack's mother hugged him tightly. "You are a brave and clever boy!" she exclaimed. "And how glad I am now that you traded the cow for those magic beans!"